The Puppy Project

"I wish I had my ~~~~~~~~~~, stuffing her han~~~~~~~~~s they walked to ~~~~~~~~~ house. "It's freezing."

Nobody came to the door when they rang the bell, but, as usual, they heard Dotty's noisy barking. It sounded even louder than usual – and closer.

"It sounds as if she's *outside*," said Neil. "Listen!"

There was another series of barks, and the scrabbling sound of paws against the back garden gate. Puppy voices yapped and whimpered urgently as Neil and Emily ran to investigate.

Titles in the Puppy Patrol® Series

More Puppy Patrol® stories follow soon

Puppy Patrol®
The Puppy Project

Jenny Dale

Illustrated by

Mick Reid

A Working Partners Book

MACMILLAN CHILDREN'S BOOKS

Special thanks to Margaret McAllister

First published 1999 by Macmillan Children's Books
This edition produced 2001 for
The Book People Ltd,
Hall Wood Avenue,
Haydock, St Helens WA11 9UL

Created by Working Partners Limited
London W6 0QT

ISBN 0 330 37632 2

5 7 9 8 6 4

A CIP catalogue record for this book is available from
the British Library.

Typeset in Bookman Old Style by SX Composing DTP, Rayleigh, Essex
Printed and bound in Great Britain by Mackays of Chatham plc, Kent

Chapter One

"Stay, Jake! Stay! Neil, hurry up! Jake won't sit still!"

"Hang on! I'm doing my best!" Eleven-year-old Neil Parker – the proud owner of a new camera – crouched down and pressed the shutter. His younger sister, Emily, laughed and shook her brown hair from her eyes as she held the wriggling puppy in her arms. Jake was a young Border collie, full of energy. Not long ago he had been soft and chubby, but he was taller now, and his black and white coat grew thicker every week.

"He wants to go to you, Neil! I think he wants to play with the camera! You're not taking another one, are you?" protested Emily.

"I'm trying!" cried Neil as he attempted to keep Jake in the frame.

It was a chilly Sunday afternoon in the exercise field at King Street Kennels, near the small country town of Compton. Emily cuddled Jake close to her chest, but when Bob Parker strode into the field with Jake's father, Sam, at his heels, the pup squirmed free and scampered to meet them.

"I brought Sam," called Bob. "I thought you'd want some pictures of him too."

Neil ran up to the two Border collies as little Jake squared up to Sam, pressing his head down between his front paws and making a noise that was meant to be a growl.

"Sam doesn't want to play," said Neil to Jake, and bent down to pat the older dog. "You'll wear him out."

Dogs were the most important thing in Neil's life. His parents, Bob and Carole, ran a boarding kennels and rescue centre at King Street as well as holding obedience classes. He loved all dogs, but Sam was his own dog, and his greatest friend. Sam looked in top condition and still loved a good run round the field, but he had a heart condition which meant that his life was constantly at risk. That was why Neil had spent some of his savings on a new camera. This way he could be sure of having plenty of pictures of Sam to keep, and of Jake too.

"Sit, Sam!" ordered Neil. Sam, who was perfectly trained, sat. "Jake, leave him alone." He took a picture just as Sam looked quizzically down at Jake as if the camera were some strange new toy Neil had just brought home. At the click of the shutter, Jake bounded up to Neil.

"Down, you daft thing! I've nearly finished the film." He threw a stick for Jake, and looked up at Emily. "I'm going to Mr Hamley's now, to take photos of Dotty's pups. Are you coming?"

"Try and stop me!" said his sister, grinning. "And if Jake won't keep still, what will Dotty's lot be like?"

Mr Hamley was Neil and Emily's head teacher at Meadowbank School. His famously naughty Dalmatian, Dotty, had given birth to eight beautiful puppies a couple of months before. Neil had helped at their birth, which made them very special to him. Five had already gone to their new owners, but three lively, lovable pups were still with their mum.

Bob looked concerned. "Why do you want to go over there?" he asked. "Now Mr Hamley's a head teacher, he'll have a lot of extra work. He'll be busy enough without you two turning up."

"It's OK." Neil whistled for the dogs and began walking back to the house. "Smiler – I mean, Mr Hamley – said I could call any time this weekend, and this is the last chance. The pups are going to their new home tomorrow."

"Rachel Hamley will be relieved," said Bob, with a chuckle. "They've got enough on their hands with the new baby to look after."

Looking after their new baby, Martin, and the wildly energetic Dotty, had been hard work for the Hamleys. So why had they decided to breed from Dotty? Neil thought people were much harder to understand than dogs.

"At least it's down to three now," said Neil. "Someone came from the Lake District for one, two are with a dog-mad family near Manchester, and the other two have moved to a stately home in Northumberland. There's just two bitches left and one dog, and he's the smallest. They call him Scrap."

"Won't Dotty miss her babies when they've all gone?" asked Emily wistfully.

"Mr Hamley says she's had enough of their teasing," said Neil. "They pull her ears and chase her tail and never let her sleep. Oh, look, isn't that Kate?"

"It can't be," puzzled Emily. "It's Sunday – her day off."

They caught sight of a tall, blonde figure as they drew near the rescue centre. Kate was the King Street kennel maid.

"She's doing so much overtime just now, she may as well move in," said Bob, and waved. There was more work than ever at King Street. The Parkers had just opened a newer, larger rescue centre with a walk-in dog clinic for local poorly pets. Kate came out to meet them; Jake jumped up at her, and the rescue dogs, hearing voices, set up a clamour of barking.

"Down, Jake!" she commanded, and bent rather stiffly to fuss him. She rubbed her back as she straightened up.

"Cleaning all those pens has done for me," she said. "I've finished here now. I'm going home for a hot megabath with half a ton of frothy stuff in it."

"You look exhausted," said Emily.

"Don't worry – help is at hand," Bob assured her. "We start interviewing for another assistant tomorrow. You'll soon have someone else to work with. It'll be good for you to have company."

"I've got lots of company," said Kate, nodding towards the pens full of dogs. She walked with Neil and Emily to the shed where the bikes were kept and they rode off together towards Compton.

Neil decided too late that ringing the doorbell at Mr Hamley's house wasn't a good idea. Dotty's loud, keen barking was soon joined by excited little yaps and then, rising louder and higher, the wailing of a baby. A door banged somewhere, steps sounded in the hall, and Mr Hamley opened the door.

He didn't look at all the way he did at school.

His face was bleary-eyed, his hair was a mess, his rumpled sweater was covered in dog hairs, and he wasn't pleased to see them. He started to say something, but was interrupted by Dotty bounding past him and nearly knocking everyone over. At Neil's command, she remembered her manners and contented herself with a noisy, licking, tail-wagging welcome.

Dotty was a mother now, but Neil wondered if she would ever grow up. She was a beautiful dog, elegant and well-balanced with dark, glossy spots. And, with her overflowing energy, she was the most uncontrollable dog Neil had ever met.

"You said we could take photos of the puppies," said Emily gently.

"Oh, yes. I suppose I did. You'd better come in." Mr Hamley led them to the kitchen. Rachel Hamley marched past with a brief nod of welcome, carrying the screaming baby Martin in one arm and a pile of clean washing in the other. In the kitchen everything seemed to be covered with a thin layer of white dog hairs, the washing machine rumbled, and piles of damp baby clothes sat next to a carton of dog meal.

The Hamleys had made a roomy pen for the puppies against the wall. There were blankets, water dishes, and some very well-chewed toys.

Putting their soft paws against the mesh, two chubby, floppy and bright-eyed Dalmatian puppies wagged their short tails in delight. They pawed eagerly at the pen, pushing little black noses against Neil and Emily's hands.

"You beauties!" cried Emily. "Aren't you growing fast!" She looked round at Mr Hamley. "But shouldn't there be three?"

"Holly's gone off exploring again," he said wearily. "The little one's Scrap, the bigger one's Berry. They've all worked out how to get out of there. No matter what we do to keep them in, they find a way round it, especially Holly. She won't stay put for five minutes. She goes off and hides in corners. I've given up even trying with her."

Neil was about to laugh, but he could see that Mr Hamley didn't find it funny. It was impossible not to laugh at Scrap, though, who was trying to chew his finger.

"No, Scrap," he said firmly. "You'll have to learn not to do that now your teeth are getting sharp."

"Can I pick them up?" asked Emily, who had already lost her heart to them.

"Yes, you may as well get them out before

they manage it for themselves," said Mr Hamley with a shrug. "You can take them into the garden for your photographs if you like."

Neil gathered a squirming bundle of puppy in his arms and glanced at his watch. "We won't be long," he said.

"Oh, take as long as you like," said Mr Hamley, sounding irritated. "You could always come back tomorrow, or the next day, or the day after that."

"What do you mean?" asked Emily, looking puzzled. "They're going to new homes tomorrow, aren't they?"

Mr Hamley rolled his eyes. "Not any more. The buyers have changed their minds. They don't want them."

"Don't want them!" repeated Neil, who could hardly believe it.

Emily, stroking Berry's smooth, warm head, looked up in amazement. "Don't want them? How could anyone not want them?" She looked down into the deep, dark eyes of the puppy trying to lick her face. "How could anyone not want you, Berry?"

"You might think they're beautiful, Emily, but the buyers – they're a family called Arkwright – they wanted show dogs. Holly and Berry looked all right to me, but now their spots are beginning to develop, they're not quite right for showing." He took Berry and ran a hand over her soft, spotted coat. "These spots are a bit patchy, really. Holly's are the same, wherever she is. Show judges like perfectly round spots."

"I don't know why they need to be so fussy," said Neil. "And Scrap's spots are perfect."

"Yes, but he's small," sighed Mr Hamley. "We were hoping he'd catch up with the others, but he hasn't. He'll always be on the petite side. Nobody will want him as a show dog . . .

Rachel's furious. She'd really counted on having the kitchen back to normal tomorrow. Goodness knows when we'll get them sold now. Do you know of anyone who'd like Dalmatian pups, Neil?"

"I was about to say," said Neil, "I can put their details on our website, if you like. That way, we can advertize them all over the country."

Neil turned his attention to Dotty as she dropped a blue rubber bone at his feet and sat back, her tail wagging hopefully. Neil threw the toy and watched the flailing welter of legs as she raced after it. He wondered if she was jealous of all the attention the babies were getting.

"Is she putting on weight, do you think?" he said.

"Could be," said Mr Hamley. "She doesn't get as much exercise as she did, I'm afraid. There isn't time for long walks any more."

"I'll take her now, if you like," said Neil. "Will you look after my camera, please? Don't let the puppies get near it!"

"I'll stay here and play with them," said Emily. She pressed her face against Berry's warm flank, then put her on the floor to play. "Were Holly and Berry called after a Christmas carol?"

11

"No, after a bush in the garden," said Mr Hamley. "It was the first thing they attacked."

"I hope they can stay together," said Emily. She looked around and then frowned. "Where's Holly?"

"I suppose I'd better go and find her," sighed Mr Hamley.

He left just in time, as Berry had been sniffing his shoelace and was about to chew it. Neil, clipping on Dotty's lead, turned to find that Scrap had followed him and was now sitting at his heels, head on one side. Neil bent to stroke the silky ears.

"Sorry, Scrap," he said, "you're not old enough for long walks yet. Stay with Emily."

"He'll follow anyone around," replied Mr Hamley from the sitting room. "He's always trotting after me and Rachel."

"That's sweet," said Emily.

"It's a nuisance," called Mr Hamley. Presently he came back in, peering in cupboards and under the furniture as he searched for Holly. "Rachel nearly broke her neck tripping over Scrap yesterday. We can't go on like this – I'm almost ready to give them away. Holly, where are you?"

"I'll give Dotty her long walk," said Neil, as

Dotty jumped up to remind him that it was time to go. "I'll try and wear her out, if she . . ."

A cry of exasperation cut him short. Mrs Hamley's voice rang down the stairs.

"Paul! I've found Holly. She's behind the dressing table. And she's taken Martin's cot blankets in there! They'll all need another wash! It's just too much!"

"Neil, I think I'll come with you after all," said Emily quickly, deciding they'd better both get out of the way. They took Dotty, and made a swift escape. Finding homes for these puppies was suddenly number one on the priority list!

Chapter Two

By the time Neil and Emily arrived back at King Street it was dark, but the lights were on at the rescue centre. They could see a car parked outside.

"That's Dr Harvey's car," said Emily. The doctor was an old friend of the family, and his two dogs had both been trained at Bob's obedience classes. There was Finn, a prize-winning Kerry blue, and a good-natured mongrel called Sandy.

The rescue centre looked bright and welcoming and, inside, still had a shiny new appearance and a faint smell of fresh paint. Dr Harvey, with his shaggy red beard and his old tweeds, was in the waiting area. Smiling, he stood up to meet them. In his arms he held a small, rough-coated mongrel with pointed ears like a fox, and he chuckled as Neil and Emily ran straight to the dog. It shivered a little, and sniffed curiously at their hands before lifting up one ear and wagging its tail.

"Who's this?" said Neil.

"Goodness knows," said the doctor. "He's a stray. He was in the middle of the road – I nearly hit him."

"You've had a lucky escape, little mutt!" said Emily. "Are Mum and Dad around?"

"Bob's interviewing a candidate for the kennel assistant's job, I believe," said Dr Harvey, scratching the little dog under the chin. One of his ears twitched forward. "When I called at the house your mum told me that some young chap had turned up for his interview today instead of tomorrow. Carole was just on her way out so I'm waiting to introduce Bob to this little stray – at least, I think he must be a stray."

He smiled warmly down at the dog, who craned his neck to look up at him. He gave a trustful wag of the tail and another twitch of the ear, and Neil scratched the top of his head. The dog twisted round to lick his wrist.

"Silly thing, running into the road like that," said Emily gently. "You could have been killed."

"That's what I told him," went on Dr Harvey. "I did a perfect emergency stop, and got out to see if he had an identity disc. The minute the car door opened he jumped up and sat in the passenger seat, asking for a ride! Anyway, he's not wearing a collar so I've brought him to the brand new five-star rescue centre."

Dr Harvey sat down, and put the dog on the floor at his feet. Neil ran his hands over the mongrel and reached into his pocket for a dog treat, which was gobbled down immediately.

"I gave him some water and a couple of dog biscuits that I had in the car," said Dr Harvey. "They vanished like snow in summer! I wonder how long he's been on the run?"

"Probably not long," said Neil. "He's a bit on the thin side, but not starving. And he's young. He still has a bit of puppyishness about him." The dog lay down, put his head on one side, twitched both ears, and stared hard at Neil's pocket.

"Just one more, then," said Neil. "I mustn't give you too much at once." As the dog crunched up the treat and put his paws on Neil's knee for attention, Neil warmed to the

16

trusting little stray, whose ears were twitching more than ever.

"He has very expressive ears, whoever he is," remarked Dr Harvey. "I wish I could do that."

Outside a door opened, and Bob appeared from the kennels office with a young man who caused Neil and Emily to glance at each other and try not to stare. It was his hair they noticed first; pink and green and sculpted into spikes. He wore a long anorak dotted with badges, purple and yellow patchwork trousers, and purple painted boots. Bob showed him out, and came back shaking his head.

"Is that your new fashion expert, Bob?" grinned Dr Harvey.

"No, and he's not our new kennel assistant either," said Bob. He looked at Neil and Emily. "And you two can stop giggling. He looks strange, but his heart's in the right place. He cares a lot about animals and he's got a brain in there. Pity he doesn't know which day of the week it is."

"You mean he didn't realize it was Sunday?" asked Emily.

Bob nodded.

"What was he like with the dogs?" asked Neil.

"Oh, no problems there. He likes them, he

17

knows how to handle them and talk to them, and they liked him. But he comes over as completely disorganized. His fashion sense might put some of our customers off too, unfortunately. The owners, not the dogs," he added, as Neil and Emily giggled again. "Dogs have more sense than people. They don't judge by appearances. Now, Alex, where did this mutt come from?"

Alex Harvey explained about the dog as Bob, talking kindly to the animal, looked at his coat and paws. The dog's ears drooped as Bob inspected his teeth, but otherwise he put up with it all patiently.

"He might be an unwanted Christmas present," said Neil.

"Mmm – I'm not so sure. It's a bit late for that. We'll put him in the rescue block." Bob patted the dog's flank. "I don't think he's been ill-kept. He didn't growl when I checked him over."

"Listen! Mum's coming home," said Emily, as the familiar note of the Range Rover's engine grew louder, and slowed to a stop on the gravel in the driveway outside. The dog stopped sniffing Bob's hands. He sat up straight. His ears twitched one at a time, then both together, and he turned his head to the sound.

Neil and Emily hurried to the door, nearly falling over the dog as he tore past them. Carole opened the car door and jumped out, and there was a burst of sudden delighted laughter.

Five-year-old Sarah, with a ribbon falling out of her hair and cake crumbs round her mouth, already had the dog in her arms. "Hello!" she giggled. "You're friendly!"

The dog wriggled free from her. He scrambled into the driving seat, put both front paws on the steering wheel, and looked from side to side.

"I think he likes cars!" said Neil. "We should call him Wheelie. Or Damon, after . . ."

"Wheelie will do," said Bob firmly. "I'm not shouting 'Damon' down the exercise field. We'll record his details and try to find out if anyone's looking for him. When Mike comes in to do the next clinic, he can check to see if he's got a microchip implant. He may even recognize him if he's local." Mike Turner was the Parkers' vet. He had a general surgery in Compton and now regularly took dedicated canine clinics at King Street. "Leave him with me, Alex," added Bob and took the little dog in his arms.

The doctor was looking intently at the top of Bob's head.

"What's so interesting?" asked Bob.

"I was imagining pink and green spikes," said Dr Harvey. "And the beard tinted to match. You should try it. It should be a nice subject for Neil's camera."

"It would break the lens," said Neil.

"And," said Dr Harvey, with a tug at Neil's short brown hair, which already stuck out in all directions, "what do you think for your brother, Emily? An apricot poodle cut?"

When Wheelie had been settled into the rescue centre and the family had finished their evening meal, Neil and Emily explained to their parents

20

about Dotty's pups and their sudden need for new homes. Jake was stretched out asleep in front of the fire, and Sam lay serenely at Neil's feet.

"The sooner they can get those puppies moved on, the better," agreed Bob. "They'll get livelier every day, and they'll get into more and more mischief as well. Yes, of course you can put the details on the website, if that's what Mr Hamley wants."

"Mrs Hamley's going out of her mind about them," said Neil. "They just seem to have taken over, and she can't wait to get everything back to normal."

"Somebody's bound to want them soon," said Emily. "They're such lovely pups."

"I wish I could see them," said Sarah.

"Unfortunately," said Carole sadly, "the world is full of lovely pups. And not enough good homes for them. I wish we didn't need any rescue centres at all." She smiled down at Sarah, who was playing with Fudge, her pet hamster.

"Fudge has forgotten all his ballet steps," said Sarah, as Fudge ran up her arm. "I'll have to teach him again. Do you get black and white spotted hamsters, like Dalmatians?"

Neil laughed.

"I don't think so, dear," said Carole. "If there is such a thing as a Dalmatian hamster I'm sure it couldn't be as nice as Fudge!" She glanced at Neil and Sarah beamed with pride.

"I sometimes think Sarah's got the right idea, keeping a hamster," said Carole. "Small pets are a lot less trouble. If Paul's willing to let us help, we'll do what we can for Dotty's pups. Three puppies, a baby, and Dotty! Poor Paul and Rachel must be going out of their minds. How on earth do they cope?"

"By the look of things," said Emily, as she stroked Jake's ears, "they don't."

"They're desperate," said Neil, "and that worries me. If we don't help them find good homes for the pups soon, they might sell to anybody, without checking on whether they'd be good owners."

When the school bell rang the next morning, Neil made his way to Mr Hamley's office. His friends Chris and Hasheem called down the corridor after him.

"Neil! Where are you going? You'll be late for registration!" shouted Hasheem.

"I need to see Smiler, about finding new

homes for Dotty's pups. If I'm late, Hasheem, can you explain to . . . um . . ." Now that Mr Hamley had been made head teacher, Neil was never quite sure who would be taking his class from one day to the next.

"Our new teacher starts today," said Hasheem. "Yes, I'll tell him – or her. See you later!"

"Hasheem!" Neil had just thought of something else. "Tell the teacher why I need to see Mr Hamley, will you? Otherwise it might look like I'm in trouble."

"Or in the doghouse!" laughed Chris.

Chris and Hasheem suddenly stopped laughing and walked sensibly to their class-rooms, so Neil knew they must have caught sight of Mr Hamley. He was on his way down the corridor looking much smarter than he had the day before, but his eyes were still shadowed and heavy. He nodded to Neil to follow him into the study, where he heaved his briefcase onto the desk and brushed a few white dog hairs from his sleeve.

"Yes, Neil, what is it?"

"I talked to my dad last night, about the puppies. We'll put their details on our website, if that's OK with you. We should get loads of interest. People from all over the country contact us about dogs."

"That's very helpful of you, Neil," said Mr Hamley. "The sooner the puppies are away, the better." The head teacher sat down behind his desk and sighed. "I don't think it was such a good idea mating Dotty when we did, you know. I had no idea how much work this lot would be – all that feeding and cleaning up. And now they want to explore all the time. They think everything's a toy."

"All dogs do that," said Neil. "They're just like little kids."

"Little kids don't eat the tablecloth," said Mr Hamley. "Berry did."

Neil smothered a laugh. "I didn't think Berry was too bad," he said. "All dogs chew things."

"Well, she's taken to scratching doors now, if she can't get to wherever Holly is. The kitchen door looks terrible. Rachel can't turn her back for a minute, without some small disaster happening. And Martin . . ." he looked at his watch. "Never mind all this, Neil. You should be in your classroom. Off you go. And don't run in the corridor."

Neil was at the classroom door before he

remembered that he didn't know who his new teacher was. Perhaps he should keep his fingers crossed. Hoping for the best and fearing the worst, he opened the door.

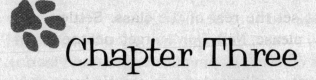

Chapter Three

A small woman with neat blond hair was sitting at the desk in Neil's classroom. She wore a smart dark suit and glasses, and looked up sternly as Neil came in.

"Neil Parker, I presume? Come here, please." Neil stood at her desk. "I'm your new teacher, Mrs Sharpe. I understand you've been to see Mr Hamley?"

"Yes, Miss."

"This wasn't on school business, was it?"

"Not exactly, Miss, but—"

"Then you shouldn't have used lesson time. Couldn't it have waited until break? Now, if you look at the board you'll see the history exercise

26

I've just set the rest of the class. Settle down quickly, please, Neil. Don't forget: neatness and accuracy."

Neil felt as if he should salute. He hurried to his place, sorted out his books, and rushed to scribble down the work on the board.

"Sharpe, as in razor sharp," whispered Hasheem. "She must have trained in the army."

"Hasheem Lindon, that's enough," said Mrs Sharpe, without even looking up. But Neil, glancing up from his work, saw a smile twitching at the corners of her mouth.

Mrs Sharpe kept the class hard at work all day. Even Mr Hamley had never been so demanding. As everyone was leaving, she called Neil to her desk.

"Neil, I need to check your address," she said. "I'm not sure if there's a mistake in this register. It says 'King Street Kennels' here. You're not a dog, are you?"

Neil grinned, and explained about the Puppy Patrol. She listened with interest, and smiled. "I like dogs, but they can be a lot of trouble," she said. "I was talking on the phone last night to my next-door neighbour from Jedburgh, where I used to live – I've just moved down here from

27

the Scottish Borders. Her dog's gone missing, and she's frantic with worry . . . Now, will you take this folder to Mr Hamley, please? We've got a staff meeting soon, and he'll need to read it before we start."

Neil met Emily in the corridor, and they went together to give Mr Hamley the folder.

"This wretched meeting," grumbled the head teacher. He looked as if he'd like to drop the folder in the bin. "It would have to be tonight. Rachel's already had all the dogs and Martin to cope with since I went out this morning. It's not fair on her if I'm late home again."

"Can we go and help?" said Emily. "We could feed the puppies, and keep them out of her way."

"And I could take Dotty for another long walk," said Neil, hopefully. "It would get her out from under Mrs Hamley's feet."

"That would be a big help," said Mr Hamley. He looked relieved. "She's at her wits' end. I'll phone your parents now and let them know where you've gone. And I'll ring Rachel, to say you're coming. Thanks. I'll get home as soon as I can."

"I wish I had my gloves with me," said Emily, stuffing her hands deep into her pockets as they walked to the Hamleys' house. "It's freezing."

They saw their breath forming chilly clouds in front of them. By the time they reached the house, Neil's ears and toes were tingling with cold.

Nobody came to the door when they rang the bell, but, as usual, they heard Dotty's noisy barking. It sounded even louder than usual – and closer.

"It sounds as if she's *outside*," said Neil. "Listen!"

There was another series of barks, and the scrabbling sound of paws against the back garden gate. Puppy voices yapped and whimpered urgently as Neil and Emily ran to investigate. It was a solid wooden gate, too high for even Dotty to jump, and with no room underneath for a small puppy to squeeze through. Dotty's head and paws popped up, followed by a row of three inquisitive little black noses under the gate, sniffing eagerly from side to side.

"That's where you are!" said Neil. "Look out for the pups, Em, don't let them run off." He opened the gate just enough to squeeze through so that Dotty couldn't run out, while Emily held on to the jostling puppies and herded them away from the gate until it was safely shut again.

"It's much too cold for them to be out," said Neil. "Mrs Hamley should be with them. Do you think she's gone out?"

"Scrap's freezing!" gasped Emily. "You come here, Scrap, and get warm." She picked up the shivering pup and cuddled him as he nestled against her for comfort. "I wonder how long they've been out here? Feel him, Neil, he's really cold!"

While Scrap huddled against Emily's shoulder, Holly and Berry had already scampered to the back doorstep, desperate to get back into the warm kitchen. They, too, were shivering as they huddled together and Holly whined softly. Berry pawed at the door, lost her balance, tumbled off the step, and clambered back to cuddle up to her sister.

"Come here, you two," said Neil. He picked up one in each arm, and they pressed against him for warmth. "At least Dotty's got a full-grown adult coat, but the pups, this isn't doing them any good!"

"What's going on?" Emily peered in at a window, trying to see any sign of life about the house. "Where's Mrs Hamley?"

"I hope she turns up soon," said Neil, shivering, "before we all freeze to death!"

As he spoke, the back door opened and Mrs Hamley appeared. She looked cross and flustered, and her hair straggled about as if it hadn't been brushed all day. On her hip she carried baby Martin, who was rubbing his eyes and looked very pink in the cheeks. Neil and Emily set the puppies down on the doorstep and the three eager little Dalmatians scuttled into the house, followed by Dotty.

Mrs Hamley looked past them at Neil and Emily. "Hello, you two. Paul just phoned to say you were coming. You could have come straight in. I wouldn't have minded." She put her free hand to her mouth to stifle a yawn. "I was too tied up to come to the door."

Neil and Emily exchanged anxious glances.

Inside, the kitchen looked worse than ever. The dogs' bowls lay unwashed beside their pen. A heap of clean nappies had been knocked off a chair and it looked as if the pups had been making a nest in them. Bits of half-eaten dog biscuit lay scattered on the floor, between two newspapers which were wet and dark in the middle. This, and the mop and bucket propped against the wall, told Neil that Mrs Hamley must have been trying to clean up puppy puddles when she put the dogs outside. She clearly hadn't wanted to risk any more. The room smelt of puppies and disinfectant.

"Holly!" snapped Mrs Hamley. Holly had returned to the nest of nappies. She stopped burrowing and looked up innocently, with a clean white nappy half over her head and half in her mouth. Neil quickly picked her up and took it away before she could do any more damage, and Emily, smiling, put out a hand towards the curly-haired baby. Mrs Hamley gently drew Martin away.

"Not when you've been handling the puppies, Emily. You can hold Martin after you've washed your hands. Put them all in the pen, please, Neil, and they might sleep for ten minutes. I wish *I* could."

"It's better if we hold on to them, Mrs Hamley," said Neil. Emily took Berry and Scrap in her arms, though Scrap struggled free and padded to Mrs Hamley's feet. "They're cold, much colder than they should be. How long were they out?"

Neil couldn't help saying it. He always thought of dogs first, and everything else afterwards. But he could see from Mrs Hamley's face that his remark had not gone down well. She pursed her lips as if she needed all her self-control not to scream. She wiped dribble from Martin's chin with a tissue. Then she turned to Neil, and the anger she was controlling glared from her eyes.

"Neil," she said, "it wasn't my idea to have Dotty mated and end up with a house full of puppies that we can't sell. Dogs may be the whole world for you, but the most important thing for me is Martin, and he takes a lot of looking after. I haven't had a decent night's sleep since he was born."

She seemed close to crying. Neil held Holly close, and looked awkwardly at the floor.

"I just hope Martin hasn't caught anything from them," she went on. "It's impossible to house-train three at once when I've got Martin to look after as well, so I'm always cleaning up after them. Everything has to be clean for babies, so I keep washing and sterilizing his toys because the dogs have got hold of them. And I tripped over Scrap this morning with Martin in my arms. He wasn't hurt, but I can't bear to think what might have happened!"

Scrap, hearing his name, looked up adoringly at her. She ruffled his ears kindly. "I'm fond of the puppies," she said, "but they're making my life impossible!"

She was trembling with rage and distress. Neil and Emily glanced at each other, unsure of what to do next.

"I'm sorry. We only wanted to help," said Neil.

"I'm sorry too." She smiled weakly. "I do appreciate your being here."

"Well, we can tidy up," said Emily, picking up a rubber bone and a tooth-marked ball. "And tell us where the cleaning stuff is, and we'll mop up the puddles. We're used to that."

"It would be a big help," said Mrs Hamley. "Then I could get on and give Martin his tea. He's starving."

She washed her hands and put a bowl of something that looked like wallpaper paste into the microwave. Then, with the bowl, a bib, and Martin, she disappeared into the sitting room. Scrap trotted after her, but Neil gently stopped him.

He soon found out what she meant about tripping over Scrap. The puppy trotted devotedly after him, sitting down so close behind him that it was hard not to step on a paw by accident. Scrap couldn't quite decide who was his best friend, Neil or the mop, but after having a good sniff at both and challenging the mop to a fight, he decided Neil smelt more interesting and sat down just where Neil would stumble over him as he turned round.

"Scrap, you daft thing!" Neil put him gently back in the pen, with a hug to reassure him that he wasn't in disgrace. "Emily, where are the other two?"

Emily looked round. "They were there a moment ago. Oh, Neil, the door into the hall's open. They could be anywhere. Let's find them quickly."

Mrs Hamley, spooning the baby food into a very messy Martin, hadn't seen the puppies either. Neil and Emily tried cupboards and corners and looked behind chairs and under beds, but with no success. Finally, Emily pointed out that the only room they hadn't tried was the bathroom.

Two guilty little black and white faces peeped out at them from the shower. Holly had pulled down a towel, and still had one end in her teeth. It trailed wetly across the floor, and a few shreds of pink sponge stuck out of Berry's

mouth. Holly dropped her towel and made one last attempt to make a nest with the shower curtain.

"Wish I had the camera," said Neil. "Come on, you pair of monkeys. No, Berry, you can't have the rubber duck. Scrap! You're under my feet again!"

They carried Holly and Berry downstairs, with Scrap following. Back in the kitchen, Dotty was wild with excitement for the exercise she needed so much. Neil treated her to a long walk, with a good run off the lead. By the time he came back, everything seemed strangely peaceful. The puppies were fast asleep, curled around each other in a warm huddle. Emily was taking a cup of tea in to Mrs Hamley.

Rachel Hamley rocked a very sleepy Martin against her shoulder. "Thanks, Emily," she said. "I think I can put Martin in his cot now."

Then, through the back door, briefcase in hand, came Mr Hamley.

Dotty set off a volley of barking so loud it was painful. Martin, startled out of his doze, screamed. Three yapping puppy voices joined in.

"Oh, *Paul!*" cried Mrs Hamley as the puppies, wide awake again, scrambled to meet him. The sudden excitement was too much for them. Almost at the same time, three puddles appeared on the floor. Neil, seeing Scrap positioning himself for something more than a puddle, grabbed him and rushed him outside.

"What's the matter with Berry?" called Mrs Hamley. "Look at her!"

From the back door, Neil could see what was the matter with Berry. Her head was down, her mouth was open, and she was straining her neck. He ran for the nearest newspaper and pushed it in front of her just in time as she emptied herself of the rest of the chewed pink sponge.

"That's better, good girl," Neil said, reassuring her. "It's all right, Mrs Hamley. She got it all on the newspaper."

"It *isn't* all right," said Mrs Hamley, pursing her lips. "That's today's paper. I hadn't read it." She looked very pale and was trembling as if she was about to explode.

Mr Hamley stood stock still – his eyes riveted on his angry wife. He smelt trouble.

Neil and Emily went very quiet.

Even the dogs quit their antics and looked up at her.

Then Mrs Hamley spoke. "I'm going to pack,"

she said quietly. "Martin and I are going to my parents tonight, and we'll stay there until this lot are all out for good. I can't stand one more day of this." And, as she strode out of the room, not even Scrap dared to follow her.

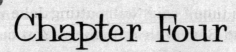

Chapter Four

N eil and Emily were halfway home before either of them spoke.

"I never thought she'd do that," said Neil at last.

"Neither did Mr Hamley," said Emily. "This is serious. We really have to get those puppies new homes."

They were soon at their own front gate, and through the kitchen window they could see Bob reaching for the oven gloves. That was a good sign. Carole was on her way across from the rescue centre with a plump, pretty girl who waved cheerfully as she walked away. As Neil opened the front door Jake and Sam raced to meet them, sniffing with great attention.

"They want to know which dogs I've been with this time," said Neil, patting Jake with one hand and Sam with the other. "You can smell Dotty, can't you, Sam?"

"I knew you'd turn up as soon as there was food on the table," called Bob. "It's ready now, so hurry up and wash."

They gathered round the table as Sarah announced that it was worms for tea, and Carole quietly told her not to make rude remarks about the spaghetti. Emily changed the subject.

"Was that girl here for an interview?" she asked.

"She was, yes," said Carole. "She's kind and good-natured, and very relaxed. But she seems too laid-back to me. We need somebody who'll keep up our high standards. We've worked hard to build up our reputation, and we can't risk losing it."

"Only the best for King Street," said Bob. "We'll see what the next one's like. How was everybody at the Hamley house?"

"How long have you got?" said Neil.

Neil and Emily told them everything that had happened, while Bob and Carole listened sympathetically. When she heard about Berry and the sponge Carole couldn't drink her tea for laughing, but she grew grave and concerned when she heard the rest of the story.

"Well! This *is* serious," she said. "It's been hard on Rachel. I know she shouldn't have left the puppies outside, but she probably didn't realize how much colder it was getting. The Hamleys had no idea what they were letting themselves in for. Babies and puppies aren't a good mix."

"You coped with it, Mum," said Neil.

"Mum copes with everything!" said Sarah.

"I've been around animals all my life," replied Carole. "And we weren't running King Street when you were born, Neil."

"You were when Sarah was born," Emily pointed out.

"Yes, but I knew which way up to hold a baby by then. And this is a purpose-built, family business kennels. We've got proper facilities and staff to make sure it runs smoothly. That's very different from one woman and a house full of puppies. Our dogs don't live in the house, except for Sam and his Lordship there." Jake looked up and beat his tail on the floor.

"Dotty's puppies are very naughty," admitted Emily. "Take Dotty, add energy, take away the little sense she's got, and multiply by three. Nothing's safe from them."

"Then I'm not surprised Rachel felt she had to get out," said Carole.

"But baby animals are sweet," said Sarah. "If Fudge met a lady hamster, they could have babies."

"Fudge wouldn't like that," said Carole quickly. "He wouldn't have all your attention to himself any more, would he? Now, if you're all finished, you can clear the table."

When the table was cleared, Neil and Bob went to the rescue centre. Neil was anxious to see how Wheelie was settling in. The little dog gave them a happy, ear-twitching greeting, and, as Neil opened the door of his pen, he brought a rubber ball and laid it hopefully at his feet.

"He's not pining, then," said Neil. He threw the ball, and Wheelie ran to pounce on it, carry it back, and drop it at his feet.

"He eats whatever I put in front of him, too," said Bob. "He's a friendly, trusting character and easily pleased. But he's a mystery. You thought he might be an abandoned Christmas puppy, didn't you, Neil?"

"Well, yes," he admitted. "But I'm not sure now."

"Mike saw him today. He reckons he's about a year old," said Bob. "That's a bit old for a Christmas puppy. He's in good condition, and there's no sign that he's ever been ill-treated. He trusts everyone."

Neil and Wheelie had a good game going by now. Neil hid the ball behind him and showed the dog his empty hands, but it didn't take Wheelie long to find it.

"But," Bob went on, "no collar, and no microchip – Mike scanned him. And no enquiries made about him."

Neil slipped the ball under his jacket, where Wheelie sniffed it out and barked to have it back. Neil threw it again. "He's been someone's friend, Dad. They must be missing him. I would, if he was my dog. I'll check the computer again, in case anybody's looking for him."

Neil looked at the website again that night. There were two enquiries about missing dogs, but neither of them answered Wheelie's description. Nobody had shown any interest in the Dalmatian puppies, either. Perhaps it was too soon. The need to find them owners was urgent, though, and would become more urgent every day that Rachel Hamley stayed away from home. When he had switched off the computer, Neil heard Carole talking to somebody over the phone.

"Yes, Paul, no problem," she was saying. "Bring them all in on your way to school in the morning. No, we don't usually take un-vaccinated pups, but, as it's you, we'll make an exception. We'll keep them in a well-scrubbed pen, isolated from the other dogs. We'll see you in the morning."

"Mum," said Neil, "was that . . . ?"

"Mr Hamley, yes," she said. "Guess who's coming to stay! With Rachel away, there's nobody at home to look after Dotty and the

Dafties, so they're coming here as boarders. I'll ring Kate tonight. She's going to love this!"

Mr Hamley arrived early the next morning, just as Kate was wheeling her bike to the shed. Neil and Emily ran outside to find her exclaiming with delight over the three puppies who pawed happily at the car windows.

"Don't let them out yet, Mr Hamley," she was saying. "They mustn't be put on the ground where other dogs have been. Here, Neil, Emily, do you want to help with this lot?"

Together they carried the delighted puppies to their designated pen. Mr Hamley had brought bedding and toys from home to help the dogs settle down in their new surroundings, and the three puppies were soon sniffing inquisitively into corners as they pattered around the run. As Bob came to join them, Dotty put her paws on Mr Hamley's shoulders for a farewell lick.

"I've checked the puppies' details on the website," said Neil. "No response yet, but we should get some interest soon."

"Don't worry about it," said Mr Hamley, taking Neil by surprise. He was a great deal calmer than he had been the previous evening, surrounded by noise and puddles. "There's a couple called Waverley-Bell who want to see them tonight."

"Who?" said Neil.

"Charles and Pamela Waverley-Bell," said Mr Hamley, with a glance at Bob. "They breed and sell pedigree dogs. One of the teachers at school lives near them and knew I wanted homes for three pups. When the Waverley-Bells heard about them they seemed really keen. Can they come here to see the pups, Bob? She sounded like a pleasant, sensible sort of person when I spoke to her over the phone."

"No problem," said Bob. "I'd like to meet them. I haven't heard that name before."

"Come on, then, you two," said Mr Hamley to Neil and Emily. "If you're ready in five minutes, I can give you a lift to school. By the way, are you keeping up with your homework? I hope all this dog-minding doesn't keep you from it."

"Of course not!" insisted Neil. With Mrs Sharpe in charge, nobody would ever dare neglect homework.

As Neil was leaving school that day, he found Toby Sparrow waiting outside the classroom. Toby's parents ran Pretty Paws, nearby. Pretty

Paws was a sort of "dog hotel" where small pedigree dogs went to be pampered, shampooed, and treated like film stars.

"I might be coming over to King Street tonight," said Toby eagerly. "Emily told me about that stray dog that jumps into cars. Mum says she'll try and get to King Street later to have a look at him, and see if she knows whose he is."

"Great!" said Neil. Relations between Pretty Paws and King Street seemed to be running smoothly now. It had been a struggle when the "doggy hotel" had first opened. Competition for King Street Kennels had made everyone feel uncomfortable. "You might be lucky, and get to see Dotty's puppies," added Neil. "They're boarding with us at the moment."

"Dotty's puppies?" Toby's eyes brightened, and a wistful look crossed his face. "Haven't they all gone yet?"

Neil knew how much Toby wanted a puppy. Not long ago he had helped to rescue three abandoned puppies, and had been heartbroken when he wasn't allowed to keep one himself. Even though the Sparrow family worked with dogs, Neil wasn't sure if Toby was ready for one of his own. He'd certainly give it love and kindness, but Neil knew that wasn't enough. He would need commitment, patience and firmness, too.

"Dalmatians are boisterous dogs," said Neil. "Look at Dotty."

"Great!" said Toby.

Neil smiled. "The thing is," he went on, "they're hard to train. And they grow big and strong, so they're not easy to handle."

"I'd learn," Toby said eagerly, and his eyes were bright. "If I had one, I'd bring it to your dad's classes. We'd practise the training every day. And I'd take it for plenty of walks."

"Even on cold mornings when it's pelting with rain and you have to take the dog out before school?" said Neil, who often had mornings like this.

"I wouldn't mind that," said Toby. "Well, maybe I would, sometimes, but I'd do it anyway. I help a lot with the Pretty Paws dogs. Neil, do you think there's any chance I could have one of Dotty's pups?"

"You'd have to ask your mum first," said Neil, carefully. "And if she did say yes, it would still be up to Mr Hamley."

Even as he said this, Neil knew that Mr Hamley was desperate enough to sell the pups to absolutely anyone. But that was the trouble.

Toby and his mother arrived at King Street in the evening, and Carole took Mrs Sparrow to the rescue centre to see Wheelie. Toby looked hopefully at Neil.

"You want to see the spotty lot, don't you?" said Neil. "Come on, then, I'll take you to the pen."

It was not long since the puppies had been fed, and they were curled in a sleepy heap of paws and ears and black button noses. Toby knelt in front of the mesh and gazed at them. Dotty, who was wide awake, bounded across, barking, to welcome them.

"Quiet! Good girl!" said Neil. "That's what they're like, Toby, when they grow up."

"Real big, doggy dogs," said Toby with longing. "Wow, Neil! Look at the pups!"

Neil looked. Disturbed by Dotty's barking, Holly and Berry had half woken up, stretched, yawned enormously, and gone back to sleep. But Scrap had noticed the visitors and was padding across the floor to them, his eyes bright and his tail wagging hard.

"His name's Scrap," said Neil.

"Scrap!" called Toby. "Come on, Scrap!"

Toby put one hand on the mesh. Scrap
sniffed at his fingers and took a lick.

"We'd better go," said Neil, suddenly feeling
uneasy. Perhaps he shouldn't have brought
Toby to see the puppies. It was love at first
sight. If Toby could have Scrap it would be one
less puppy for Mr Hamley to worry about, and
the fulfilment of Toby's dreams. But could Toby
provide a good home for a growing dog? And
would his mother allow him to have a puppy? If
not, he would be heartbroken.

Chapter Five

"Are you still in there?" called Carole. "Time to go, Toby."

Toby tore himself away from the dogs in the rescue centre, still gazing over his shoulder on the way out.

"Mum . . ." he began, but his mother stopped him.

"I know what you're going to ask. And I'm not making any promises. We'll talk about it, that's all," she said firmly.

Neil and Carole watched them go.

"Did she recognize Wheelie?" asked Neil.

"No, didn't have a clue about him," said Carol. "But she's much more doggy-minded since she's been doing her kennel management course. If Toby did get a puppy, she'd make sure he took good care of it. Hang on, who on earth is this?" she added, as a very smart Range Rover swished into the drive.

"Someone with a brand new car," said Neil. "And Mr Hamley's in it!"

They could already see Bob on his way to greet the new arrivals. As Neil approached he could hear Mr Hamley, who was smiling broadly, introducing his new friends.

"Charles and Pamela Waverley-Bell," he said. "They're interested in buying the puppies."

The Waverley-Bells, smiling and friendly, were already shaking hands with Bob. Both were very well-spoken. They were about fifty, plainly but smartly dressed in tweedy clothes. The man was tall and wore a cap and a waxed jacket, and Mrs Waverley-Bell was a squarely built woman with neatly styled greying hair and sensible shoes. Neil joined the group as they went with Mr Hamley and Bob to the boarding kennels. Mr Hamley looked very pleased with himself.

"You're new to this area, I think?" said Bob.

"Yes, we've just moved to one of the big houses on Riverside Road, just on this side of Colshaw," said Mr Waverley-Bell. "We needed a place with outhouses to convert into kennels."

"I've seen the kennels," said Mr Hamley quickly. "They're very clean and comfortable."

"And what breeds do you deal in?" asked Bob, leading the way to Dotty's pen.

"Oh, a wide range," said Mr Waverley-Bell. "Westies, chihuahuas, retrievers, and Dalmatians, of course. It's difficult to run a successful business by specializing in just one breed. We prefer to offer our clients choice. Dalmatians are very popular just now."

They reached Dotty's pen, and Neil expected to see the usual smile of delight when anyone saw the puppies. Bob opened the door and, as Dotty hurled herself at Mr Hamley, Neil watched the Waverley-Bells.

Without saying a word, they bent down and picked up a puppy each. With careful attention Charles Waverley-Bell held Berry in one arm while he inspected her teeth and ran his free hand over the shape of her head. She took a playful lick at his wrist, but he ignored her.

"Mmmn," was all he said.

Pamela Waverley-Bell was examining Holly's paws with great care. Scrap nestled in Neil's arms, looking up at his face. For a pen full of puppies, it was strangely quiet.

Mr Waverley-Bell spoke at last. "She has a jolly nice head," he said. "It's a pity about her markings. She's a strong pup, though."

His wife held Holly at a distance to take a better look at her.

"Will this one be good enough to breed from? That's the question," she said. "I wonder how she'll turn out when she's fully grown? As you say, the markings are patchy. Hardly any spots on her tail, which is rather a shame." She balanced Holly's tail in one hand, then passed the puppy to Neil with a polite smile, and took Scrap. In her large hands, he looked tinier than ever.

The way they handled the dogs baffled Neil. They may as well have been holding two suitcases, or two bags of shopping. The Waverley-Bells weren't unkind, or careless. They handled the puppies expertly, checking their bone structure and their markings. But neither of them spoke to the pups. They didn't bother to make friends with them, or calm them. There was no stroking, no fuss, no play. They didn't even smile. How could anyone hold Scrap and not smile?

Neil glanced up at Mr Hamley and tried to catch his eye, but he was looking at Scrap in Pamela Waverley-Bell's efficient hands. Dotty stood beside him, unusually still and controlled, observing all that happened.

At last, the Waverley-Bells looked at each other, and both raised their eyebrows.

"We'll have to talk it over," said Mrs Waverley-Bell. She put Scrap on the floor, and he immediately scampered to Neil's outstretched hands.

"I see," said Mr Hamley. "Well, thanks, Bob. We'll get out of your way now."

Neil was still thinking of the bright, longing face of Toby Sparrow. He urgently needed a word with Mr Hamley in private.

"Mr Hamley, will you just have a quick look at my homework, please?" he said. "It's really important."

Mr Hamley put Holly on the floor and followed Neil outside.

"Is it really homework that's suddenly so important, Neil?" he asked.

"No, Mr Hamley, but I had to talk to you privately," he said. "I don't like the look of them. They're not taking any real interest in the pups."

"They look very interested to me."

"Yes, but they don't treat the pups as—" Neil nearly said *people*, "as *personalities*. They don't look as if they really *care*."

"You may see it like that, Neil. But to me, they just look like professionals."

"And there's something else," said Neil. "Toby Sparrow was asking about the puppies today. He'd love one."

Mr Hamley looked surprised. "I had no idea about that. Has his mother agreed?"

"No, but she might," insisted Neil. "She said they'd talk about it."

Mr Hamley smiled kindly. "If I know Mrs Sparrow, I'm afraid he won't have much success. I don't think she'd let him have anything that grows to Dotty's size, or with her energy, to say nothing of her gift for making chaos."

A soft growl came from somewhere in the pen. They looked round the door in time to see Dotty take Berry gently by the scruff of the neck and lead her back to the bedding.

Neil dodged out of sight of the door.

"Dotty doesn't like them, either!" he whispered.

"Dotty's behaving badly just now, you know that," Mr Hamley whispered back. "She might be wrong about them, and so might you. I don't have a lot of choice, Neil. Now, I mustn't keep them waiting."

Mr Hamley turned on his heels and left Neil alone with his fears.

Neil watched the gleaming Range Rover drive away. It was smart and well-maintained. It looked as if it belonged to people who knew what they were doing and had their lives well organized. But that didn't make them good puppy owners.

"Dad," he said, "I didn't like the look of them. They didn't seem to care about the dogs."

"I know what you mean." Bob fingered his

beard thoughtfully. "But maybe that's just their manner. They want to look businesslike. And it's up to Paul Hamley, not us."

Neil remained worried and miserable until he opened the front door and was met by Jake and Sam, falling over each other to greet him. He always felt better after a thorough welcome from his dogs.

"Mum's gone back to the rescue centre," said Emily, without looking up from her homework. "She's showing another candidate round. If you're going up there, say hello to Wheelie for me, will you?"

Neil was already out of the door when he decided to go back for the camera. He knew that having films developed was an expensive business and that he couldn't afford to photograph *every* dog at King Street, but he'd grown attached to Wheelie.

He hurried towards the warm glow of the rescue centre and headed straight for Wheelie's pen, making a big fuss of the affectionate little mongrel. Wheelie had his usual game with the rubber ball, then Neil took the camera from his pocket.

"Smile, Wheelie!" he said.

But Wheelie was already sitting up smartly,

as if he'd been ordered to. His ears lifted. As soon as the shutter clicked he padded up to Neil, sniffing hopefully at the pocket where the dog treats were usually kept.

"Good dog!" Neil tickled him under his chin where his collar should have been, and gave him a biscuit. "You know all about cameras, don't you? Someone must have taken a lot of pictures of you. They must be missing you."

He put the precious camera carefully in its case and into his pocket. Wheelie brought the rubber ball and was clearly hoping to play again, but there were other dogs Neil wanted to say hello to. He gave Wheelie one last pat.

"They must be searching everywhere for you," he said. "They're sure to find you."

He had looked in on two or three other dogs when he saw Carole leaving the office and walking towards him. There was a small woman with her who was as slender as a dancer. She had a bright, lively face. As Carole moved out of the way, Neil saw Sarah. She was holding the woman's hand and gazing lovingly up at her. Whoever she was, she'd made a big impression on his little sister.

"Hi, Neil!" called Carole. "Come and meet Bev. Bev, this is Neil, my son."

Bev smiled broadly. The dog hairs on her clothes showed that she had already come into contact with the occupants of the kennel blocks. Inside the rescue centre, a dog in the nearest pen trotted to the mesh to see what was going on and Bev knelt down and held out her hands towards him, looking carefully at his eyes.

"Looks like cataracts to me," she remarked.

"Yes, advanced cataracts," said Carole. "But he's old, and they don't bother him, so Mike doesn't want to operate. You should see the Afghan in the next pen. She's a beauty."

"Oh, yes!" said Bev, moving on to admire the sleek and graceful Afghan hound. "Isn't she splendid? I reckon people buy these dogs because they look so stylish, then they find out how much grooming they need. Can be a bit snappy, can't they, Afghans?"

"Never look them in the eye," said Bob, as he arrived to join them. "This one, as you say, was brought to us by an owner who found he just couldn't cope with all the grooming and walking. If you come to work here, grooming Natasha may well be one of your first jobs."

"Have you got dogs?" asked Neil.

Bev's face lit up. "Oh, I've never been without a dog in the house. The one we've got now, Milly, she was a rescue dog from here."

Neil remembered the pooch from a couple of years back, but didn't remember Bev.

"Black and tan mongrel," Bev continued. "Most intelligent dog I've ever had. Which is your favourite, Sarah?"

"Wheelie," said Sarah at once. Then she thought again. "Or Scrap. Maybe Berry. I'm not sure. All of them!"

When the Parkers were all in the house and Bev had gone, Carole flopped wearily into an armchair and looked up at Bob.

"I think she's the one," she said.

"She's pretty good, isn't she?" said Bob. "She looks a bit waif-like, but I think she's tough."

"She's worked as a nurse, so she must be," said Carole. "And she's obviously a very caring person."

"She seems to know a lot about dogs," added Neil. "She looks as if she feels at home with them."

"She's lovely," said Sarah. "I told her all about Fudge, and she said she used to have a hamster called Twitch. And the dogs all liked her."

"Yes, they did," said Carole. "She said she's always wanted to work with animals but never had the opportunity before. Now her family are all grown up, and she's free to give it a go. We talked about qualifications, and she's already done her Kennel Staff Certificate."

"Pity Kate wasn't here to meet her," said Bob. "Still, I expect they'll get on. She can start next week, and I'd be really glad of that. There's enough work on at the moment to keep an army busy."

"Her references are excellent," said Carole. "She's got enough sense and initiative to see what needs doing, and to do it. Yes, I think we should offer her the job."

"Good," said Neil, "I'm glad that's sorted. But aren't we forgetting something?"

Everybody exchanged puzzled looks.

To Neil the answer was obvious. "Dotty! We still haven't done anything about Dotty's pups! If we don't find homes for them soon, Mr Hamley might end up selling them to those Wobbly-Bell people!"

Bob scratched his beard. "Hang on a minute, Neil—"

Neil interrupted him. "I know what you said, Dad, but I wouldn't trust them with any dog. Not even a toy dog with batteries in!"

Chapter Six

"What's all this about?" asked Carole. Neil and Bob told her about the Waverley-Bells and their visit to view Dotty's three energetic offspring.

"Just because they didn't get down on their hands and knees to play with the puppies," said Carole, "that doesn't make them heartless. They have their licence to breed dogs, haven't they?" Neil was about to ask her what sort of licence they needed, but Sarah distracted everybody with her continuing stories of how wonderful Bev was. Then Emily piped up about her concerns over finding Wheelie's owner.

"When you get your pictures developed, Neil," she was saying, "we could scan the best one and put it on to posters. And put it on the website, too. The way he keeps hopping into cars, he could have come from anywhere in the country."

"Well, he certainly isn't local," said Neil. "I think he would have been claimed by now."

"But if you left a car door open, and a dog jumped in, you'd know about it, wouldn't you?" went on Emily, thinking out loud. "You couldn't just drive off without knowing he was there. Unless he got into a van of some sort, or a trailer, and got out again as soon as it stopped. He could be from anywhere, Land's End to thingummy Groats, for all we know."

She went on talking about Wheelie, but Neil didn't hear any of it. He was aware of Jake and Sam, under the table at his feet. Not long ago, Jake had been as small and vulnerable as Dotty's pups. He wouldn't have wanted anyone to handle him the way the Waverley-Bells had handled Holly, Berry, and Scrap, without even a pat or a kind word. Finally, unable to shake off the worry, he slipped out to the boarding kennels.

"No, Dotty, you're not going anywhere," he said, patting the huge Dalmatian as she leapt to greet him. "I just need to think."

He knelt on the floor, with Scrap settling down in his lap. He kept one arm across Dotty's warm, smooth back and stroked Holly's head with his free hand. The gentle, repeated stroking of the soft fur helped him to concentrate.

Carole had said something about breeding kennels needing a licence. He knew there was a law about that. He just couldn't remember what it was. It might be worth finding out, though.

"Down you get, Scrap," he said, gently lifting the sleepy pup from his lap. "I'll see you lot in the morning."

He found Bob in the office, studying a spreadsheet on the computer.

"Dad?"

Bob swung round in the office chair. "You're still worrying about those puppies, aren't you, Neil?"

Neil nodded gloomily, and Bob went on, "Do you really think you'll be happy, Neil, whoever takes them? I'm glad you care so much, but I do wonder if you're getting too attached to them."

"It's not like that, Dad. I just want them to be happy. But I really came to ask you about licences."

"Oh, yes, for a breeding kennel. If they have more than two bitches, they have to apply for a licence. One of the conditions of having and keeping a licence is that they have to be inspected by the local authority."

"So if they don't have a licence, they're breaking the law?"

"Yes, but who says they don't? They seem pretty organized to me. I suppose it might be worth mentioning it to Terri, in case she wants to check them out." Terri McCall was the local RSPCA inspector. She and the Parker family had often helped each other out in the past.

"Can I check the website, Dad?" asked Neil.

"Just in case anyone's asking about the puppies?"

"Yes, I've finished here anyway," replied Bob, closing down his program files then standing up and shuffling his paperwork together.

Neil sat down at the computer, logged on to the Internet and clicked in to the King Street Kennels e-mail system. Fairly quickly his face erupted into a wide grin. "Dad, there's someone out there who wants the pups! There's a name and a phone number and an e-mail address! Quick, let's get straight back to them!"

"Slow down," said Bob. "Give me the details."

Neil hurriedly scrawled the name and numbers on the back of an envelope and thrust them towards his dad.

"Copper . . . what does that squiggle say?" Bob asked as he tried to read what Neil had written. He looked more closely. "It isn't Copperthwaite, is it?" Then a broad grin spread across *his* face too, and he chuckled. "Not Jeremy Copperthwaite?"

"Yes, that's it," said Neil. "Jeremy and Sally Copperthwaite, it says here."

"Carole," called Bob, running outside.

Neil followed him into the house.

"Carole, come and see this!" cried Bob up the

69

stairs. "Jeremy Copperthwaite's got his eye on Dotty's pups!"

"Not *the* Jeremy Copperthwaite?" asked Carole, who had been putting Sarah to bed.

"How many Jeremy Copperthwaites can there be?" asked Neil, sarcastically.

Bob couldn't stop smiling. "Well, if Jeremy wants them we needn't look for anyone else." He grinned at Neil. "I was at college with Jeremy. He came from the West Country, but he married a lass from Derbyshire, and the last I knew about them they were settling down there, with a boarding kennels and training classes. Probably the best dog handler I ever knew. Mind, he didn't keep Dalmatians then."

"Well, it sounds as if he wants to now," said Carole. "And they couldn't go to anyone better. We'll give him a ring."

There was only an answering machine at the number Bob phoned. He left a message on it, and Neil sent an e-mail.

"It'll be good to see Jeremy and Sally again," said Bob. "I'll tell Paul Hamley that I can personally recommend them."

"Do you suppose the Copperthwaites will want all of them, Dad?" asked Neil.

Carole laughed. "If Toby wants one, he can

always ask Paul to keep one for him," she said. "So long as he and his mum make their minds up quickly."

Things were moving fast, thought Neil. A couple of days ago, the Hamleys seemed to think they'd never find homes for the puppies. Now, there was a choice of offers. He thought he'd better phone Toby.

There was only an answering machine at the Sparrows' number, so Neil left a message. "Hi, Toby, it's Neil," he said. "If you do want a pup, you'd better move fast. See you tomorrow."

Hoping he wouldn't get another answering machine, he decided to phone Terri too. He was relieved to hear her kind, reassuring voice as she answered the phone.

"Neil! Good to hear from you. What can I do?"

Terri listened while Neil explained about the puppies and the Waverley-Bells. When he had finished, she said, "So there's no actual cruelty going on, as far as you know?"

"Well, no."

"No neglect? Nothing likely to cause harm?"

"Nothing like that – at least, nothing I know about."

"And you haven't seen their kennels?"

"No, but Mr Hamley says they're very good.

It's just the way they are with the puppies. I know it sounds as if I'm phoning you for nothing, but . . ."

"If in doubt, Neil, always phone me," she said firmly. "Now, the name Waverley-Bell means nothing to me, but I'll make some enquiries and see if any of my RSPCA colleagues know anything about them. And I'll find out if they have a licence. How are Jake and Sam doing?"

"They're fine. That reminds me, I think it's time I let Jake into the garden. Bye, Terri, and thanks. Call me soon."

He found Jake sitting hopefully at the back door so he let the dog out, and stood waiting in the doorway. Jake sniffed about, chose a bush, watered it thoroughly, and scampered back in again.

"Good dog," said Neil, giving Jake a pat and a ruffle of the ears. He couldn't imagine life without a dog. He thought of Toby Sparrow, who wanted one so much.

"There has to be a puppy for Toby this time," he said to Emily when he found her reading in the sitting room. "He really wants one, and he'd be a good owner."

"Wouldn't he like a rescue dog?" said Emily.

"I think he's set his heart on a certain

72

Dalmatian puppy," said Neil. "He's aiming for the best."

"I'm more worried about Wheelie," said Emily. "Do you think we should make some posters? We'd need thousands. And even so, we couldn't cover the whole country. I just hate to think that we might never get him back together with his owner. It would be terrible for both of them."

"Keep looking, Em," said Neil. "You'll crack it."

Neil struggled to wake up the next morning. Through a deep sleep he could hear car doors banging, and the barking of a dog. He drifted into a dream in which Wheelie jumped into the Waverley-Bells' Range Rover and drove it away with Dotty and the puppies in the back. But there were voices outside, and the feeling that something important was happening pulled him out of sleep. It was unusual to hear this amount of activity so early in the day. Struggling awake, he pulled on his clothes and ran downstairs.

Sarah sat at the kitchen table, sticky with marmalade. "Morning, Neil!"

"Wotcha, Squirt," Neil managed. He fidgeted

and looked around nervously. "Have I missed anything?" he asked.

Sarah giggled. "No! Only your head teacher."

Neil was surprised. "What? Mr Hamley was here? What did he want?" But he didn't stop for Sarah's answer – even if she knew. Suddenly *he* knew exactly why Mr Hamley had visited them so early.

He lunged for the kitchen door and ran all the way to the boarding kennels.

His heart was pounding.

Surely it couldn't be true.

Neil scrambled through the door of Kennel Block One, barged past his dad – who he nearly knocked over – and hurried to the end pen.

It was empty.

Dotty and her pups had gone.

Chapter Seven

A tuft of white fur lay on the floor of Dotty's pen. Neil picked it up, wondering which of the pups had shed it. As he did so, he realized that Bob was behind him.

"Mr Hamley came early this morning," he said. "He's sold the puppies already, to the Waverley-Bells. I'm sorry, Neil, but it's out of our control. They're not our dogs."

The worst thing about working with dogs was parting with them. Neil had often had to do that before, but he still hadn't got used to it. This time he found himself empty and aching, knowing that he'd never see Holly, Berry and Scrap again. He wouldn't even have the satisfaction of seeing them go to kind, understanding owners who could make them happy. And how was Toby going to feel?

For once, Neil was speechless. He just nodded to his father and left for school soon after breakfast. He wasn't very hungry.

Arriving at school that morning, Neil felt that nothing could be worse. But it could. Toby Sparrow ran to meet him, his eyes shining, his voice gabbling with excitement.

"I can have a puppy! Mum says I can have one of—"

"Toby," said Neil with a heavy heart. He couldn't bear to let him go on. Toby saw the misery on his face, and his smile vanished.

"What's the matter? Is it the puppies? Are they all right?"

"I'm really sorry, Toby," said Neil. He felt wretched. "Mr Hamley's already sold them." He glanced away as Toby struggled to control his shaking lower lip.

"It's not your fault, Neil," he muttered. Then he rubbed his sleeve across his face, and ran. Neil would have followed him, but, at that moment, the bell rang.

"Neil?" Mrs Sharpe called his name as he and Hasheem walked into the classroom.

"Neil, are you all right?"

Neil was still upset and angry, but he hadn't meant to let it show. "Yes, miss," he said. She looked at him for a moment, and he knew she didn't believe him.

"Well," she said, fussily brushing something off her neat red suit, "Mr Hamley would like to see you at morning break."

Neil didn't want to see Mr Hamley. Perhaps he shouldn't blame him for selling the pups to the Waverley-Bells. Poor Mr Hamley couldn't have a normal family life again until the puppies were gone. And now they were. For ever.

At break, he made his way to the office.

"Neil," said Mr Hamley. His voice was unusually gentle. "Sit down."

As he sat, Neil thought about what it must be like at Mr Hamley's house now. Dotty must be all alone and Neil couldn't imagine going back there. It would be too quiet with no yapping pups, no Holly and Berry playing hide and seek, no Scrap to trip over. He could visualize the kitchen, with the pen dismantled and the bedding washed and neatly folded away. He thought of the day he had watched Dotty give birth to those puppies. He'd miss them terribly. Especially Scrap.

"I'm sorry about the pups," said Mr Hamley. "I realize you must be upset."

"If you'd just waited a bit longer, we had other buyers lined up for them," said Neil. "One of dad's friends. And Toby."

"Yes, Neil, but I didn't know that when I made my decision. You didn't know it either, did you? And I really didn't think Mrs Sparrow would let Toby have one."

"You could have asked them to wait," said Neil. He couldn't help it. "You could have talked to my dad."

"I was desperate, Neil, and the Waverley-Bells were prepared to pay at once and take them straight home. They offered me less than I'd asked, because of the markings, and because Scrap is so small, but what could I do? I really didn't care about the money. Rachel had been pushed out of her own home."

Neil nodded. "Is that all?" All of a sudden, he was desperate for some fresh air.

"Yes – but, Neil, don't worry about the Waverley-Bells. I know you didn't like them, but they seem to know what they're doing. I'm sure they're all right."

There was no point in arguing. Neil went out to the playground. He saw Chris and Hasheem talking to Toby Sparrow and Emily. Chris was giving Toby a friendly pat on the shoulder, and Hasheem was offering him a sweet. As Neil joined them he saw that Toby looked pale, and was still a bit pink around the eyes.

"I wish you could have had one of them, Toby," said Neil. "I did what I could."

Toby nodded bravely. "Mum might let me have a rescue dog, anyway," he said. But Neil knew he had set his heart on a Dalmatian puppy. When the bell rang, they headed for their classrooms.

"I suppose he'll get over it," said Hasheem. "What are they like, those Wobbly-Bells or whatever they're called? They sound dead posh, with a name like that."

"Their Range Rover's a lot smarter than ours," said Neil. "Newest model, latest registration."

"Really?" said Chris. "I've seen one like that. It often goes past our place. I noticed it because it always has dog stuff in it."

"Are you sure?" asked Neil.

"Positive. I'm sure I've even seen the odd dog being ferried around too. It only appeared very recently. It's usually parked on Riverside Road, outside that big red-brick house. That's not far from Toby's place, is it?"

"Might be worth looking at," said Neil, before he and Emily went to their different classrooms. "What do you think, Emily?"

"Hurry up, Neil!" whispered Hasheem. "We daren't be late for anything these days! Sharpe's the word!"

Neil and Emily didn't usually sit together at lunchtimes, but today they somehow ended up at the same table. Mrs Sharpe, carrying a plate of cheese flan and salad, came to join them.

"Is there room for another one?" she said, smiling. She always sat with the pupils, never with the teachers.

"There's a seat here, miss," said Emily, and moved her plate along a bit.

Neil looked around the room to see who was looking at them. Sitting with a teacher was seriously uncool.

However, as Mrs Sharpe began to talk, he found her really surprising. She was as strict as a sergeant major in class – nobody dared to step out of line – but she was friendly and good-natured, too, especially out of lesson time.

"What sort of dog do you have, miss?" asked Emily.

Mrs Sharpe laughed. "You two live and breathe dogs! I don't have one. Not everyone does!"

"There are dog hairs on your sleeve," Emily pointed out. "I just thought . . ."

"Oh, that!" Mrs Sharpe turned her arm so she could see, and picked a few stray hairs from her suit. "It's a complete mystery. Ever since I moved in I've been finding dog hairs – mostly on the furniture, but they seem to end up on my clothes, too. I don't understand it."

Emily carefully picked a hair or two from the

red sleeve. She inspected them in her fingers, and held them up to the light.

"What's so interesting?" asked Neil.

"Probably nothing," said Emily innocently, and went on eating her lunch.

After school, Neil and Emily cycled up to Riverside Road. There was no sign of the Range Rover, but they found the house Chris had talked about. It was tall and spacious, with a neatly tended front garden and elegantly draped curtains at the windows. A gravel path led down one side of the house to the garden and outhouses behind it.

"Neil! What if somebody comes?" said Emily.

Even as she spoke, a car drew up. Neil stopped, but, to his relief, it wasn't the smart Range Rover. The car parking outside the house was a red Metro, and a young woman in a tight dark suit stepped out. She smiled at Emily.

"Are they not here yet?" she said. Her manner was bright and easygoing. "They told me to come at four. This is the right house, isn't it? The Waverley-Bells?"

"Yes," said Emily. "But I don't know . . ."

"Are you getting a little puppy too?" She smiled brightly. "I saw their advert in the paper.

They've got chihuahuas, and I think they're so sweet! So they said to come here at four o'clock, and they'd have one ready for me."

"As simply as that?" said Neil. "Didn't they want to know anything about you?"

The woman laughed. "Why should they need to know anything about me?" She glanced at her watch. "I was afraid I'd be late. I've just been to the library to get a book about dogs. I thought I'd better find out a bit about looking after them."

"Shouldn't you have done that sooner?" demanded Neil, but she only gave an awkward little laugh.

"My friend got a puppy from here," she said. "They're really good here. She said the kennels were lovely, all nice and clean and roomy. What sort of puppy are you getting?"

"We're not buying a puppy today," said Emily. "It's time we went, Neil. We can't do anything more here just now."

"Oh, did you just come to have a look at the little puppies?" chirped the young woman.

"Yes, I suppose we did," said Emily, "but we're not staying."

"Just a minute," said Neil, and he turned to the woman. "It's not a good idea to buy a dog until you really know what you're letting yourself in for. They're a lot of work, even little ones, and you need to know about how to care for them. But if you must get a puppy today, take it to Mike Turner, the vet in Compton. He'll check it over and give it its injections, and advise you about it."

The woman looked quite bewildered.

"Trust us," said Emily, "we know what we're talking about. Come on, Neil!"

"So that's how they do business," growled Neil as they wheeled their bikes away. "They don't care who they sell to. Any airhead who can read an advert in a newspaper can just turn up and buy a puppy. It's like a supermarket."

A small figure on the other side of the road waved at them.

"There's Toby!" said Emily, waving back.

"Not again!" said Neil. "I can't get away from him today."

"What's the matter with Toby?" demanded Emily crossly.

"Nothing. I just feel so rotten about seeing him, because of the puppies." But Toby had already crossed the road to talk to them, looking as bright and hopeful as he had first thing that morning, when he still hoped for a

Dalmatian puppy of his own.

"Neil, Em, I've had a great idea!" he announced. "At least, it might be a daft idea, but you won't laugh, will you?"

"Let's hear it, then," said Neil.

"The people who bought Scrap," began Toby, "they bought him to breed from, didn't they? I want a puppy of my own, and I want one like Scrap, and I don't mind if I have to wait, even if I have to wait for years and years. When Scrap's old enough to breed from, there'll be puppies, and maybe I can buy one of those! What do you think, Neil! Son of Scrap!"

For Toby's sake, Neil gave an encouraging nod, but he wasn't really thinking about Toby's idea. A completely new thought had occurred to him.

"It's possible, Toby," he said, "but it would be a long wait. Emily and I have to get home now. Bye!"

"Em, I've just realized something," he whispered urgently, as soon as Toby was out of the way. "I should have seen it at once."

"Surprise me."

"The Waverley-Bells want dogs to breed from, right?"

"Right."

85

"But they said it themselves – Scrap's undersized! That's why they offered a low price for him! Who wants to breed from the runt of the litter?"

"What about breeding from Holly and Berry, then?"

"I'm not sure. Maybe they're good breeding stock, but Scrap certainly isn't. They don't want to breed from him, they want to sell him." Neil was on a roll now. "And, judging by what we've just seen, they couldn't care less who they sell to. I bet Mr Hamley wouldn't be so happy knowing that Dotty's pups could be going to irresponsible owners!"

"So?" asked Emily.

"So we need to get them back," replied Neil. "Fast!"

Chapter Eight

Neil and Emily arrived home at King Street just in time to meet Bob on his way back from walking two large, glossy black Labradors who were boarding at the kennels. Neil went with him as he took them back to their pen.

"Dad," he said, "I've just found out something about the Waverley-Bells." As they filled the dogs' dishes with water, he told him about the young woman who had arrived to buy a puppy.

"They were going to sell her a puppy there and then, no questions asked," concluded Neil. "They knew nothing about her and she knew nothing about dogs."

"Maybe," pondered Bob. "But perhaps they'd

suss her out at that first meeting and decide whether to let her have a puppy or not."

"Huh!" countered Neil, grumpily.

"I agree, it's not a good way to sell dogs."

"But that's not all," said Neil. Bob locked the door and they walked down to the house. "Toby Sparrow said something that set me thinking. He was talking about how Scrap would father a litter of puppies one day, and he might be able to have one."

"He'd have a long wait!" laughed Bob.

"That's not the point. We've been missing something all this time. Scrap isn't the kind of dog you would breed from, is he, Dad?"

"I see what you mean," said Bob, and tugged thoughtfully at his beard. "You could be on to something there. Scrap's a smashing little pup. He'd make someone a perfect pet. But he's not a stud dog."

"So why did they want him? Do you suppose they're going to sell him?"

Bob was quiet and thoughtful for a few seconds. Then he said, "I think that must be it. They've bought him for a knock-down price so they can sell at a good profit. You're right, Neil, we should . . ." Bob hesitated. "*I* should have seen that earlier."

"So they lied to Mr Hamley," said Neil grimly.

At the front door, Jake and Sam raced to meet them. A delicious smell of cooking beckoned from the warm kitchen.

"What about Holly and Berry?" said Neil. "Do you suppose they'll sell them, too? They did say that their markings were poor."

"That may just have been an excuse to force the price down," said Bob. "Mike and I were just talking about this. You know about the problems with breeding dogs to show standard, don't you, Neil?"

"Yes, you end up breeding in bad points as well as good ones," said Neil, pleased to show that he understood. "So if a dog has a good point, like perfect markings, that can be passed on to its pups. But it'll pass on weaknesses, too, like poor eyesight or nervous temperament."

"Right. Dalmatians sometimes have problems with their hearing. There's been too much effort over the years to breed Dalmatians with perfect spots, and they've ended up producing dogs with poor hearing. So we now have a lot of perfectly marked Dalmatians going deaf."

"There's nothing the matter with Holly and Berry's hearing," chuckled Neil. "They know all about the doorbell!"

"So they could be good breeding bitches," said Bob. "Anyone with a bit of sense would want a generally healthy dog, rather than a perfectly marked one. They might breed from them, or they might sell them, I can't be sure. But I'm sure about Scrap."

"We need to tell Terri," said Neil.

"What can she do?" said Bob. "They've been dishonest, but not cruel."

All the same, Neil rang the RSPCA inspector's number. She sounded out of breath when she answered the phone.

"I've just got in from one call," she gasped, "and I have to dash out to another. Is it about the new kennels in Colshaw?"

"Yes. I think they—"

"Don't worry, Neil, I'm following it up. I'll be in touch soon. I have to go now – I have a cat to rescue. Bye!"

Neil put the phone down. He wished he'd been able to explain more to Terri about the Waverley-Bells although, as Bob had pointed out, there was no reason to think they'd been cruel to any animal. At least she was already on the case. He still felt uneasy, though.

He found Emily sprawled on the sitting room floor, reading the *Compton News*. Jake, who

seemed to think this was some sort of game, tried fighting with the paper and, when Emily stopped him, he took a good lick at her instead.

"Behave, Jake!" she said, and, giving in, she stood up and lifted the paper from the floor. "Look at this, Neil. In the adverts."

Neil took the paper and read out the advertisement she was pointing to. "*Puppies – Westies, chihuahuas, retrievers, Dalmatians, ready now*," he read. "And there's a Compton phone number, but no name. This must be the Waverley-Bells. And it sounds like a big operation. If they go on like this, Compton will be full of dogs belonging to clueless owners."

"Exactly!" said Emily.

"Well," said Neil defiantly, "I don't want Scrap to be one of them."

Neil went to bed that night still anxious about the puppies. It wasn't just Dotty's puppies any more, but all the litters in the Waverley-Bells' kennels. He slept badly, and woke while it was still dark, knowing that he couldn't get back to sleep even if he tried. He decided he might as well get up, and take the dogs out.

Quietly he pulled on warm clothes, went downstairs, and whistled for Sam and Jake, who were delighted to have an early walk. Jake galloped from one clump of grass to the next, snuffling into every corner. Sam, after an initial burst of energy, settled down to a trot at Neil's heel.

Turning up his collar against the cold, Neil wondered how long it might be before Scrap was sold. There didn't seem to be much he could do to prevent it, but if he could just be there, at the kennels in Riverside Road, at least he'd know what was going on. Perhaps he could do something if he was on the spot.

He turned for home, and saw that the light

was on in Emily's room. He found her dressed, and putting her shoes on.

"You going out already?" he said.

"I couldn't sleep. I thought I may as well go up to the rescue centre."

"How about coming with me instead? I'm going to pay a call on the Waverley-Bells."

"It's a bit early, isn't it?"

Neil thought for a moment. "Well, by the time we've grabbed something to eat and walked up there, it won't be 'a bit early', will it? We *have* to go up there. We can't just leave things as they are. At least, if we can find out a bit more about them, I can report back to Terri and give her something to work on."

"So what do we do?" demanded Emily. "Turn up on the doorstep and say, 'Hi, we're checking you out to see if we should report you to the RSPCA?' We have to have some reason for being there. I wonder if we could pretend to be choosing a puppy?"

"I don't suppose even they would sell to somebody our age," said Neil. "And I was here when the Waverley-Bells came to look at the puppies. They might remember me."

"Your face isn't that funny," said Emily. "They were looking at the puppies, not you.

93

Let's go round there and say . . . Oh, what can we say . . . ?"

"Got it!" said Neil, as inspiration struck. "Let's say we want to help with the dogs! Tell them we love animals and we heard about the kennels, and we want to help. Then we can get a good look at how they do things."

"And see Dotty's puppies," said Emily.

"And get some evidence for Terri," said Neil. "Just hold on a minute, Em."

As Emily put on her jacket, Neil went to find his camera and the last spare film. He had a feeling they might be needed.

Chapter Nine

Neil and Emily stood on the doorstep of the elegant house in Riverside Road. When the door was opened, Emily put on her most appealing smile.

"Hello, are you Mr Waverley-Bell?" she asked. "This is where the new kennels has just opened, isn't it?"

"It certainly is." He smiled down at her. "Did you come to buy a puppy? You'd have to bring your parents with you, you know."

Neil gritted his teeth, but Emily kept her wide-eyed, innocent expression.

"No, we don't want to buy one," she said, "but we'd like to help with them. We're very experienced with dogs."

"We thought you might want some help with feeding and cleaning out," Neil added. "Like my sister said, we're used to doing that."

Mr Waverley-Bell looked carefully at Neil.

"Haven't I seen you before?" he said. "Weren't you at King Street Kennels the other day, when we went to look at some puppies?"

Neil was about to deny it, but he thought twice.

"Yes," he said. "We help out there, too."

"But it looks really, really good here," said Emily, quickly changing the subject. Just then, there was a call from the top of the stairs.

"Charles, have you done the nine thirty check?" It was the loud, no-nonsense voice of Pamela Waverley-Bell as she hurried down-stairs. "We've got buyers coming all morning, we have to make sure we're all spick and span for . . . oh! Visitors already? I'm afraid you're too early to see the dogs."

"We're here to help," said Emily quickly.

"They tell me they do have experience," added Mr Waverley-Bell, who seemed to like the idea of having help at the kennels.

"We just like helping with dogs," said Neil.

"Well, if you're not afraid of hard work, we do need all the help we can get," she said. "We might even pay you something if you're as good a help as you say you are. Welcome aboard. Charles will show you the kennel block. Oh, and Charles . . ."

She lowered her voice, but Neil and Emily heard what she said to him.

"Charles, if that silly girl does come back, try and sell her a chihuahua this time. I don't know why she was so dithery yesterday. I told her she'd have to let us know for definite this morning whether she's buying or not."

Neil and Emily exchanged glances as Charles Waverley-Bell led them down the path to the back of the house. There was a clean yard, fenced on three sides, with a row of outhouses on the fourth.

"This would have been a stable and storage space at one time," said Mr Waverley-Bell, opening the door of the long, whitewashed building. "We converted it into a kennels. I think you'll be impressed."

They were. It was a well-lit building, with spacious pens against the wall. Opposite the pens, there were shelves on which packets of dog food, dishes, and cleaning fluids were neatly stacked. Mops and brushes stood in a corner.

"It's almost as good as King Street!" whispered Emily.

Neil hadn't imagined anything like this from the Waverley-Bells. At least it meant that the puppies weren't suffering from bad conditions. He followed Charles Waverley-Bell as he patrolled along the long row of pens.

"Two retrievers in here, twelve weeks old, one dog, one bitch," he said, pointing to a pen as he walked past it. "Chihuahuas in here, three bitches, one dog, ten weeks old. Westies, three, two dogs, one bitch, ten weeks. Three Dalmatians – but you know about those, don't you? In the adjoining room" – he opened a door – "three breeding bitches, one retriever, two Westies, all expecting litters within the next couple of weeks."

Neil was already kneeling in front of the Dalmatians' pen. The puppies ran to him with little yaps of greeting.

"Hi, Scrap!" he said. "They must remember me – from that day at King Street," he added quickly. "Hello Holly, hello Berry, you pair of scamps!"

"Don't fuss them," ordered Mr Waverley-Bell. "It doesn't do to get too fond of the dogs. This is a commercial kennels, run to make a profit. The

98

dogs are here to be sold or bred from. Mostly, we don't even need to use their name."

Emily was on her knees in front of the chihuahuas.

"They're no bigger than frogs!" she said. "They're gorgeous! Look, Neil, they're so sweet!"

Neil tried to agree that they were "sweet", but couldn't quite manage the word. "They're nice dogs," he said.

"That's right, but don't get sentimental about them," said Mr Waverley-Bell. He walked past the pens without a glance at the puppies pawing and yapping at the mesh, and pointed out a chart on the wall.

"They were all fed and the pens cleaned at seven thirty this morning," he said. "The nine thirty check is to fill the water dishes, check all the puppies are well, and clean the pens again. We have to be very thorough on a Saturday, when we have more customers than usual. Feeding again at eleven thirty, cleaning at two, cleaning and feeding at five and eight. Pens are cleaned one at a time, and the dogs put in the yard while the pens are being washed down."

"Don't you ever play with them?" said Emily.

Mr Waverley-Bell frowned. "They're not toys," he said. "Look sharp, now, before the customers arrive. Start with Pen One – that's the retrievers – and work your way along. Tick the chart on the wall when each pen has been done. And please be sure that the dogs are looking their best, would you? Customers arriving soon!"

With that, he returned to the house. Neil and Emily mopped and scrubbed and shook out the bedding and, knowing that the Waverley-Bells were out of the way, made a fuss of the pups. Neil took a surreptitious look at a pile of papers on the office desk. There were various notes scribbled down on different pieces of paper.

"Look at this!" he said, craning round and reading aloud from the notes. "It says, *Dalmatian dog, too small – sell. Chihuahuas, two larger bitches, poor bone structure – sell, don't breed.* I'll photograph that. This looks like pretty dodgy business to me."

"I suppose it's all right if they're honest with the buyers," said Emily, "and tell them that the dogs have faults. If they try to pass them off as excellent show dogs, then it's dishonest."

Neil took his photograph and knelt on the floor beside the Westies. Their stubby tails were wagging furiously.

"They're desperate for attention," he said.

Then he jumped to his feet, put his camera behind his back and tried to look busy as Mrs Waverley-Bell strode in.

"I've got someone arriving soon to buy a retriever bitch," she said, and looked thoughtfully into the pen. "I'll offer the smaller one. The other will do for breeding."

"Pamela," called her husband. "We have a visitor."

Mrs Waverley-Bell turned sharply and strode out to the yard.

"Do you have an appointment?" she asked.

"No," replied a woman's voice, "but I would very much like to see you."

"That's Toby's mum!" whispered Emily.

"Stay out of sight," Neil whispered back. "I want to see what happens." They stood to one side of a window and watched as Mrs Sparrow told the Waverley-Bells why she was there.

"My son had his heart set on a Dalmatian puppy," she explained. "I did intend to buy it for him, but I learned too late that you'd bought it to breed from. My son wanted him so much, I wonder if you'd consider selling him?"

"That's a mistake," whispered Neil. "If they know she really wants him, they'll push the price up."

"A Dalmatian pup," said Mrs Waverley-Bell, thoughtfully. "Yes, I know the one you mean. I'm afraid, Mrs . . . er . . ."

"Sparrow," she said.

". . . I'm afraid, Mrs Sparrow, you put me in a difficult position. The dog is a valuable stud dog. We're very keen to breed from him. He has an excellent pedigree and some fine qualities."

"What a whacking great lie!" whispered Emily.

"A good pedigree? Oh. I didn't think he was that valuable. I know a little about dogs myself, I—"

"No, he's worth a lot of money," interrupted Mr Waverley-Bell.

"But you do have two bitches with the same pedigree, too?" asked Mrs Sparrow.

"Oh, but what we really needed was a stud dog," Mrs Waverley-Bell said firmly. "I wish I could help you. I'd hate to think of the child being disappointed, but we have a business to run."

"I can't believe this!" muttered Neil.

"What a shame, though," went on Mrs Waverley-Bell, "about your little boy. I wonder, Charles, could we let the Dalmatian go?"

"We have to consider what we paid for him," he said, "and the cost of buying another dog as good as this one."

"Yes, I understand that," said Mrs Sparrow.

"I suppose," he went on, "we could just about afford to let him go for – what do you think, Pamela? – for three hundred and fifty."

"What!" whispered Neil.

"I'm sorry," went on Mr Waverley-Bell, "but he's really worth more."

"That's not what they told Mr Hamley," whispered Neil to Emily. "He said they gave a low price because Scrap was a runt."

"Excuse me, I think there's someone at the door," said Mr Waverley-Bell. He gave a charming smile. "It may be the young lady who wanted a chihuahua." And he left his wife with Mrs Sparrow.

"I'm sorry," said Mrs Sparrow. "Three hundred and fifty is impossible."

"I wonder." Mrs Waverley-Bell seemed to be hesitating. "Perhaps we could go down to three hundred and twenty. I'd have to ask Charles."

"This can't go on!" Neil muttered fiercely. "She's trying to force Mrs Sparrow to pay the earth for him, and just for greed! And I'm not going to stay here and watch a rip-off!" He marched out into the yard.

"Hello, Mrs Sparrow!"

"Neil Parker!" she exclaimed.

"Have you two met?" demanded Mrs Waverley-Bell. She looked quickly from one to the other with suspicion in her eyes. "Is something going on here? What's that in your hand?"

Neil had forgotten that he was still holding his camera. He took a step away from her.

"I can't have you coming in here and taking photographs! Hand that over!"

"It's my camera!" protested Neil, but she made a grab at it all the same.

There was a cry of "Leave him alone!" from Mrs Sparrow, and "Stop it!" from Emily as Neil backed away and Mrs Waverley-Bell reached for the camera. From somewhere on the path, there was a call of "Pamela!" and, turning at the sound of her name, she lost her footing, stumbled heavily, and grabbed at Neil.

Neil was knocked off balance. There was a crash and a splintering of glass.

Mrs Waverley-Bell struggled to her feet. Neil stood looking at the smashed camera on the ground, not quite able to believe what had just

happened. For the moment, he was too stunned
to be angry.

Then, walking purposefully down the garden
path, wearing her RSPCA uniform, came Terri.

Chapter Ten

"This lady," said Charles Waverley-Bell, "is Terri McCall, from the RSPCA." He was still smiling warmly, but Neil could see the anxiety in his eyes. He cast a puzzled glance at the broken camera on the ground, but was more concerned with Terri.

Mrs Waverley-Bell ignored the camera, and the bewildered Mrs Sparrow. She extended a hand to Terri.

"Very nice to meet you," she said. "I'm sure you'll find everything here in order."

"It certainly looks very efficient," said Terri, glancing through the open door at the pens and the puppies. "May I see your licence, please?"

"Where is our licence, Charles?" asked Mrs

Waverley-Bell, after the tiniest pause. "I think it's in the desk, isn't it? I know it should be on the noticeboard, but we've only just opened these premises." Neil could see she was desperately playing for time.

"Don't you remember, dear, we had to return it?" said her husband. "They made a mistake with . . . er . . . the address, so we sent it back and asked for a replacement."

Terri stopped smiling. "Perhaps I should come to the point," she said. "No application has been received. You haven't applied for a licence to breed dogs. I've checked with the council."

"It must have been lost in the post," suggested Mr Waverley-Bell, still trying to rescue the situation.

"You do realize," said Terri, being firm but very polite, "that it's illegal to set up a breeding kennels without a valid licence."

The Waverley-Bells looked at each other. Mr Waverley-Bell tried a different tactic. "Yes, but that's not really something that concerns you as an RSPCA inspector, is it? I mean, what you really came about, my dear, is the welfare of the dogs, and you can see that they are extremely well cared for here. We can dispense with all this silly form-filling business, can't we? I'm sure you have more important things to do than chase around after licences."

Terri held her ground. "I have to uphold the law," she said. "You are trading in animals without a licence. As you did when you were based in Kent, using the name Pamela Bell, when the council ordered you to close down your kennels."

In spite of the disaster with his camera, Neil felt a smile tugging at the corners of his mouth. Terri had done her homework.

Pamela Waverley-Bell was growing red in the face.

"That's just typical," she snapped. "All we want to do is run a business. We're efficient, we're well organized, and we work extremely hard. And you want to deprive us of our livelihood for a silly detail like a licence. We're getting one, of course. We've just been too busy doing more important things, like looking after our dogs. We're trying to make a living, and what's the matter with that?"

"You don't care about your dogs," said Neil, and everyone turned to look at him. "That's what's the matter. You think the most important thing in all this is the money you make. You only take care of the dogs because you want them to fetch a good price. You don't care about them as dogs. Real, live dogs, with feelings."

"Well said, Neil!" said Mrs Sparrow.

"I must ask you both to cooperate," said Terri to the Waverley-Bells. "You are not really in a position of advantage. This is the second time you have failed to purchase a licence for a business of this nature."

"Is there anybody around?" called a voice. Neil and Emily recognized it at once. So did the three Dalmatian pups, who started a chorus of excited little yaps and cries.

"Over here, Mr Hamley!" called Emily.

Mr Hamley strode down the path, his face set and grim. Neil knew that look. It meant someone was in big trouble.

"This is ridiculous!" complained Mrs Waverley-Bell. "It's like Trafalgar Square here today!"

"Good morning, Terri," he said briskly. "Neil, Emily, I might have known you'd turn up. Mrs Sparrow, good morning! Now, I'll come straight to the point." He turned to face Mr Waverley-Bell. "I've brought back your cheque. I wish to withdraw from the sale, and I want the puppies returned to me at once."

"I'm afraid that isn't possible, Mr Hamley," he said. "The deal has gone through. I'm not prepared to go back on it. Those dogs belong to us now."

"You won't be allowed to keep them, Mr Waverley-Bell," Terri pointed out. "It would be better for you to return them now. At least this way you'll get back the money you paid for them."

Neil was impressed. Terri had known the question of money would bring the Waverley-Bells to their senses.

"It's not at all businesslike," sighed Pamela Waverley-Bell. "But I suppose it will have to do."

"Neil, I'm sorry," said Mr Hamley. "You know, I was already having second thoughts about the puppies before Terri phoned me to ask me about the details of the sale. I wish I'd listened to you in the first place."

He took a cheque from his wallet and pushed it into Mr Waverley-Bell's hand. "Would you fetch the puppies, please, Neil?" he said. As Neil and Emily ran to the pen, neither of the Waverley-Bells made any attempt to stop them.

"Come on then, you," said Neil, as the puppies jumped and clambered around him,

110

their tails wagging and their tongues licking eagerly. "Let's get you out of here." He handed Scrap to Emily, and carried Holly and Berry out himself, one under each arm. "Are you taking them back to King Street, Mr Hamley?"

"I'd like to, if you still have room for them," he said. "Rachel's just moved back in, and I don't want her to move straight out again."

"Excuse me, Mr Hamley," said Mrs Sparrow. "Is Scrap still for sale? Mr and Mrs Waverley-Bell were asking three hundred and fifty, which I thought was—"

"They asked *how* much?" gasped Mr Hamley.

"We have to make a profit," snapped Mrs Waverley-Bell.

"That's a great deal more than they paid me for all three of them together," said Mr Hamley, in a voice of frightening quietness. "Charles, Pamela – you are simply the most dishonest people I have ever done business with. Neil and Emily, would you take the puppies back to the car, please?"

"Just a minute," said Neil. He handed Holly to Emily and bent to pick up what was left of his camera. "Somebody will have to sweep up there, otherwise you might get a puppy standing on broken glass."

"Neil!" exclaimed Mr Hamley. "That's not your new camera, is it?"

"It was." Neil shrugged. "There was an . . . accident. Don't worry though," added Neil, biting back his disappointment. "The puppies are all right, and I've still got my film with the pictures of Sam and Jake. Those are the really important things." And he smiled down into Berry's face.

"I want to have a word with these people before I go," said Mr Hamley. "But I'll unlock the car first, and you two can hop in."

"Oh! That reminds me," said Emily, as they went with him to the car. "Dogs hopping into cars! I'd almost forgotten about Wheelie!"

"What about Wheelie?" asked Neil, as they settled themselves in the car with the dogs on their laps.

"I think I know who he belongs to! Remember, Mrs Sharpe told you that her old next-door neighbour, from Jedburgh, had lost her dog? And Mrs Sharpe had dog hairs on her suit. She said they were on her furniture, and she couldn't understand how they got there. I think Wheelie must have arrived in Compton in a delivery van. Mrs Sharpe's delivery van!"

"So Wheelie gets out, has a lift in the van – probably falls asleep on Mrs Sharpe's settee – and jumps out when they get here! Nice one!"

"I checked it out," she said. "I kept some of those hairs from her suit and compared them with Wheelie's. They're a perfect match. The only thing I don't have is a description of the missing dog from Jedburgh. If Mr Hamley can give me Mrs Sharpe's phone number, I can ring up and ask her what he looked like."

"You're going to make someone a very happy owner," said Neil, grinning.

The following afternoon, everything became even busier than usual at King Street Kennels. Neil, arriving home from walking Jake and Sam, found Mrs Sharpe just arriving, and Mrs Sparrow's car already parked on the drive. And there was another car, which Neil couldn't remember seeing before. He could see his parents outside Kennel Block One, chatting away non-stop to two visitors.

"I'll take you to meet Mum and Dad," said Neil to Mrs Sharpe. "I don't know who that is with them."

He was able to guess pretty soon, though. There was a big, fair-haired man and a woman with a kind face. She held Holly and Berry in her arms.

"Hi, Neil!" called Bob. "Come and meet Jeremy and Sally. They're taking Holly and Berry."

"Lovely pups, aren't they?" called Jeremy Copperthwaite. "A pair of rascals – just the way we like them!"

"Great!" said Neil. "But what about Toby?"

"Look in there," said Bob, and nodded towards the door.

Jeremy chuckled, and murmured something about a sight worth seeing.

Neil went inside. In a corner, curled up on the floor, was Toby, with a tail-wagging, licking, little Scrap in his arms. With shining eyes, Toby looked up at Neil. "He's mine," he whispered, as if he couldn't quite believe it yet. "Really mine." He looked down adoringly at Scrap, who stretched up and licked his nose. "He's brilliant. He's my best friend."

Neil nodded. He knew what that felt like.

Bob appeared at his side. "It's a good job you discovered what you did about the Waverley-Bells when you did or this might not have happened."

Neil smiled. "They won't be able to buy and sell dogs any more now, will they?"

"It's unlikely. This latest offence won't have done them any favours at all. This business is better off without them."

"You can say that again." Neil didn't want to take himself away from the sight of Toby and Scrap, but he knew that Mrs Sharpe would still be waiting to see Wheelie. Back outside though, he found Carole already escorting Mrs Sharpe to the rescue centre, and ran to catch up with them. He thought it would be worth seeing what happened next.

Above the barking of the rescue dogs came a

cry of joy from Mrs Sharpe. "Wiz! It really is you! Barbara will be so glad!"

"He's called Wiz?" asked Neil. "'Wheelie' wasn't too far off the mark, then!"

Carole, smiling, opened the pen, and Wheelie immediately brought his favourite rubber ball to play with. Mrs Sharpe played Fetch with him as she talked.

"When Emily rang to say you had a dog that might be the missing one from Jedburgh, I rang Barbara, my neighbour, to let her know. She said it was the most terrible day when he disappeared. She'd taken his collar off for a bath, then someone came to the door, and the phone rang, and somebody must have left the gate open. The next thing she knew, she couldn't find him anywhere. She had adverts for him all over the Borders, but she never thought of looking this far. She said to pass on her thanks to you for taking such good care of him."

"He's been a model visitor," said Carole, grinning, as Emily arrived to join them. "Emily was the one who worked out where he came from."

"If you can keep him here until Friday," said Mrs Sharpe, "I'm going back to Jedburgh for the weekend and I'll take him home. Barbara says she'll be sending a cheque to the rescue centre and that she's going to have him fitted with a microchip."

"If he's going to keep hitching lifts, it might be a good idea!" said Carole.

"It's his only bad habit," said Emily. "He's very well-behaved. A lot better than these Dalmatian puppies!"

Neil walked away, meaning to join Toby and Scrap. For Toby, there was nothing in the world better than a Dalmatian puppy.

As he left the rescue centre though, he saw someone else arriving. Bob was already on his way to meet the new visitors.

"I should build a multi-storey car park," he was saying. "Oh, it's the Hamleys! And they've brought Martin." He waved in greeting. "Hi, Paul, Rachel. Would you like to come in the house?"

"I blame myself for all this," said Rachel. She seated herself at the kitchen table, with the baby in her lap. Sarah ran to put her finger in Martin's hand, and he chuckled at her. "If I hadn't walked out like that, Paul wouldn't have been so desperate to sell the pups."

"It's not your fault," said Mr Hamley. "Things

were just completely out of hand, and you'd had all you could take. Do you know, Neil, when I told her what had happened she chewed my ear off and said she hadn't intended me to sell them to just anyone like that! Can't win, can I?"

"You'll just be in time to say goodbye to the puppies if you want to," said Neil, stroking Sam's ears.

"Before we do, Neil, we've got something for you," Mr Hamley said. Mrs Hamley reached into her bag and brought out a gift-wrapped parcel.

"That's from all of us, including Dotty," she said, smiling, as she handed it to him. "It's to say thank you for all your help. We know you could use one."

Neil pulled off the paper and dropped it on the floor where Jake immediately tore it to shreds, but, for once, Neil barely noticed the young Border collie. In his hands he held a new, stylish, state-of-the-art, out-of-this-world camera, complete with film.

"Thank you," he said. "Thank you very much."

Gasping his thanks and almost shaking with joy, he loaded the film and knelt down.

Jake looked up, a bit of wrapping paper hanging out of his mouth. Neil pointed the camera.

"Smile, Jake!" he said.

Look out for Puppy Patrol® No. 22:

Superdog!

Simply the best!

Superdog is a brand new competition for dogs of all shapes and sizes. And Twister is a natural winner. He's fast, he's clever, he's adorable – and Neil and Emily think he's top dog.

But it's tough at the top, and Twister faces stiff competition – from some very determined dog-owners. Can the Parkers help Twister prove that he really is the best?

Look out for Puppy Patrol® No. 23:

Sherlock's Home

Will he make the grade?

Sherlock is strong, intelligent and reliable – perfect qualities for a would-be police dog. But there's one problem – his owner is an ex-thief!

When Sergeant Moorhead begins his search for a new dog, it's up to Neil and Emily Parker to persuade him that Sherlock is the right dog for the job . . .